SCHOLASTIC INC.

New York   Toronto   London   Auckland   Sydney   Tokyo

# THE ADVENTURES OF
# THE GET ALONG GANG

By MARY SWENSON
Illustrated by NEAL McPHEETERS

ISBN 0-590-33186-8
Copyright © 1984 by American Greetings Corp. All rights reserved. Published by Scholastic Inc.

12 11 10 9 8 7 6 5 4 3 2 1     5     4 5 6 7 8/8

Printed in the U.S.A.                     10

The Get Along Gang,™ Montgomery "Good News" Moose,™ Dotty Dog,™ Zipper Cat,™ Woolma Lamb,™ Bingo "Bet-It-All" Beaver,™ Portia Porcupine,™ Rocco Rabbit,™ Flora Fox,™ Braker Turtle,™ Lolly Squirrel,™ Rudyard Lion,™ and Bernice Bear™ are trademarks of American Greetings Corp.

Every year the small, pleasant town of Green Meadow held a big festival. The Festival included a car race, known as the Grand Prix. To the citizens of Green Meadow, it was a grand event with a grand prize—a big silver cup. Each year the members of the Get Along Gang talked about entering the race in their very own car. Each year, however, they ended up entering the Scavenger Hunt instead.

One afternoon the Get Along Gang met at the Clubhouse Caboose for one of its weekly meetings. "The first order of business," said Montgomery Moose, the unofficial leader of the gang, "is this year's Green Meadow Festival."

"I move that we enter the Grand Prix this year," said Portia Porcupine. Portia, the youngest member of the gang, liked to be a part of things: road races *and* club meetings.

Bingo "Bet-It-All" Beaver, who was always ready for a little excitement, seconded the motion. "Well, why don't we do it this year?" he said. "Why don't we show this town that the Get Along Gang can win the Grand Prix?"

The rest of the gang stared at Bingo as if he had just suggested a snowball fight in July.

"For the same reason we didn't enter the race last year," said Zipper Cat. "Or the year before that. *We don't have a car.*"

"Oh, yeah," said Bingo, looking down at his sneakers. "I always forget. But Montgomery knows how to drive, and Dotty knows about car engines. Don't forget that." Dotty Dog, the mechanical wizard of the gang, looked over at Bingo and smiled.

Montgomery shook his head. "I suggest that we enter the Scavenger Hunt instead," he said. "It's on the same day."

"You always suggest that because you always win," complained Zipper. Every head in the clubhouse turned to look at Montgomery's collection of Scavenger Hunt blue ribbons. Montgomery looked a little embarrassed.

"It doesn't matter who wins," said Dotty Dog, "as long as the whole gang has fun."

Dotty Dog was working on her latest invention. No one was sure what it would be. She asked Montgomery to hold the old bagpipe that she was trying to attach to part of a bicycle. Dotty liked to make new things out of old parts and pieces. "And it's not the blue ribbon that's important," said Dotty, tightening a bolt with her wrench. "It's the fun of trying to win it."

"I'd have more fun trying to win a *pink* ribbon," said Woolma Lamb, patting her curls, "a dark pink ribbon like the raspberry sherbet at Hoofnagel's Ice Cream Emporium. Now, that's my color!"

Bingo snapped his fingers. "I've got it!" he cried. "What if there were a different prize this year, something bigger and better?"

"Like *two* blue ribbons?" asked Portia.

"No! Better than that!" said Bingo excitedly. "What if Hoofnagel's Ice Cream Emporium sponsored the Scavenger Hunt—and the prize was ice cream?"

"Mr. Hoofnagel would never give away ice cream," said Portia. "He's too cheap."

Woolma gasped at Portia's choice of words and covered her ears. "You don't say *cheap,* Portia," explained Woolma. "You say *stingy* or *miserly* or *penurious.*"

Portia looked surprised. "I do?"

"I'll go talk to Mr. Hoofnagel right now," said Bingo. "Just leave it to me."

"Wait, Bingo," said Montgomery. "I think someone should go with you—to make sure that you don't get us into any trouble."

"Trouble!" cried Bingo in a shocked voice. "I dare you to name one time that I got the gang into trouble."

Voices exploded as everyone in the clubhouse began naming *all* the times that Bingo had gotten them into trouble.

"Hmmmm," said Bingo, studying his sneakers again. "I guess I *have* caused a few difficult moments. Dotty, can you...um... go with me to Hoofnagel's?"

Hoofnagel's Ice Cream Emporium had a long name but a short list of customers. When Bingo and Dotty dropped by that afternoon, the store was almost empty. Bingo ordered a milk shake and Dotty asked for a sundae. They sat on stools at the soda fountain and watched Mr. Hoofnagel count peanuts. Mr. Hoofnagel always put ten peanuts on a sundae—no more, no less.

"Just think, Mr. Hoofnagel," said Bingo, "if you sponsor the Scavenger Hunt, you'll be famous."

"I don't want to be famous," replied Mr. Hoofnagel abruptly.

"Everyone in Green Meadow will say that you are a pillar of the community," Bingo continued.

Mr. Hoofnagel set the sundae on the counter and handed Dotty a spoon. "I don't want to be a pillar of the community," he said.

"Look at it this way," said Dotty. "When people hear that you sponsored the Scavenger Hunt, they'll come *here* to buy their ice cream."

Mr. Hoofnagel stopped to think about Dotty's last point. "Let me see if I have this straight," he said. "If I sponsor the Scavenger Hunt, you say I'll have more customers. And if I have more customers, I'll sell more ice cream. I can go one step further. If I sell more ice cream, I'll make more money."

"That's right," said Dotty. "But you should offer an interesting prize for the Scavenger Hunt. Like an ice-cream flavor named in honor of the winner."

"Agreed," said Mr. Hoofnagel.

"*And,*" Bingo added quickly, "as many free milk shakes as he or she can drink."

"I don't want to agree to that," said Mr. Hoofnagel, "but I'll do it anyway."

When Bingo and Dotty returned to the clubhouse, the Get Along Gang gathered around to hear the news.

"Imagine an ice cream named after me," said Woolma.
"Woolma Whip Supreme,
The most beautiful ice cream."
"Or one for me," said Flora Fox. "Flora's Framboise Flip!"

"How about Rudyard's Fudge?" suggested Rudyard Lion.

"Or Lolly Squirrel's Lemon Swirl?" said Lolly Squirrel.

"All I know," said Zipper Cat, "is that I'd like Zipper Ripple much better than Mocha Moose. It's time I started to make my name known."

While the members of the Get Along Gang were imagining themselves as ice-cream flavors, Mr. Hoofnagel was driving his ice-cream truck up and down the streets of Green Meadow to advertise the Scavenger Hunt—and, of course, his personal contribution.

"Remember, folks," said Mr. Hoofnagel's voice through the loudspeaker, "if it wasn't for Hoofnagel, there would not be a

super-special Scavenger Hunt. So when you want ice cream, hoof it down to Hoofnagel's Ice Cream Emporium. Hoofnagel —a pillar of the community!"

As the ice-cream truck passed Gummyfoot Swamp, a crocodile named Catchum and a lizard named Leland were just crawling out of the water. They listened with interest to the news about the Scavenger Hunt.

As they were wringing swamp water out of their clothes, they too began to think about ice cream. "Imagine everyone in town asking for two scoops of Catchum Crocodile Crunch!" said Catchum.

At that very moment, Catchum heard a distinct crunching sound and felt a distinct crunching sensation. It was his tail. When he looked down, he discovered that Leland was wringing *it* out too.

"And imagine everyone asking for three scoops of Leland Lizard Lime," said Leland.

"Stop twisting my tail, you lean-witted lizard!" cried Catchum. "I'm trying to think."

Leland stared at Catchum's tail with a new sense of awe. So *that* was where Catchum kept that marvelous brain of his.

"How would you like to join in the fun, my dear boy?" said Catchum in his most devious voice.

"You mean join the Get Along Gang?" asked Leland. "They're the ones who always enter the Scavenger Hunt, Boss."

Catchum suddenly looked ill. "I will not join a gang that insists on 'getting along,'" he said. "But, as I always say...if you can't join 'em, beat 'em."

Leland looked at Catchum as if Catchum had just suggested going for a swim in January. "Beat the gang?" said Leland. "But there are so many of them—and just two of us."

"That's right," said Catchum, grinning. "But we cheat!"

On the morning of the Scavenger Hunt, which was also the day of the Grand Prix, the sidewalk in front of Hoofnagel's Ice Cream Emporium was lined with wooden bins. Each bin had a name on it—so that each contestant would have a place to put the things he or she found during the hunt. A list of the items to be found was hidden under a large white sheet.

All but two contestants were inside the store listening to Mr. Hoofnagel read the rules of the contest. Catchum and Leland were outside, hiding behind the bins.

"The Get Along Gang doesn't suspect a thing, do they, Boss?" said Leland, snickering. "They're probably thinking that we could never win because we're too lazy, too dumb, too....By the way, Boss, how *are* we going to win?"

"Simple," said Catchum. "I will add one more item to the list, and I will be the only one who understands what it is."

Leland looked worried. "You can't add anything to the list," he said.

"Why not?" asked Catchum, suddenly scared that Leland might know something he didn't know.

"Because," said Leland, "the list is covered up."

"Wake up your brain, you reptilious runt," said Catchum. "You're missing the important stuff. Just keep your eyes open, and let me know if you see anyone."

Catchum pulled out his marking pencil, crept over to the large white sheet, and disappeared under it.

Leland did keep his eyes open. He looked all around as if he were suspecting trouble. He looked up the street. He looked down the street. Then he happened to look at the large white sheet. An unusual bulge seemed to be moving under it.

"Hmmmm, I wonder what that strange bump is," Leland said to himself. "I'd better have a little peek." He walked over to the sheet and lifted one corner.

"STOP!" cried a gruff voice. "STAY AWAY FROM THAT SHEET!"

Leland let go of the sheet and turned around. The bulge under the sheet froze. There stood Officer Growler, who was the judge for the Scavenger Hunt.

"Who, me?" said Leland.

"Who else would I mean?" asked Officer Growler. "Nobody is allowed to look at that list until the contest officially begins."

Officer Growler went over and threw open the door of the Ice Cream Emporium. He did not see Catchum Crocodile slip out from under the sheet.

The entire Get Along Gang came rushing out of the store at ninety miles an hour. Then they tore down the sheet and began reading the scavenger list.

Officer Growler, who had failed to step out of the way before the stampede, picked himself up off the sidewalk and wobbled to safety. "The contest has officially begun," he announced weakly.

Mr. Hoofnagel was the last one out of the Emporium. "I'm going to have a lot of customers today," he said. "I need to get more ice cream." He jumped in his truck and drove away.

Everyone studied the list. Each item on it was worth a certain number of points.

"It's nine o'clock," said Montgomery. "We have until twelve noon. Then the one with the most points wins."

"I know where I can find an air compressor pump," said Dotty.

"I have a birchbark canoe at home!" Zipper exclaimed. "It's worth two hundred and ten points."

"The last item is worth the most points," said Braker Turtle. "A lacer...tilia squa...mata. I should know what that is, but I don't. What is it?"

"Beats me," said Bingo.

"Who cares?" said Woolma. "I know what I'm going after—the full-length mirror!"

Everyone hurried off to start hunting.

## GREEN MEADOW FESTIVAL DAY SCAVENGER HUNT

| | POINTS | | POINTS |
|---|---|---|---|
| AIR COMPRESSOR PUMP | 60 | CHICKEN DENTURES | 5 |
| LAMP SHADE | 5 | ELECTRIC POGO STICK | 30 |
| BALL OF TIN FOIL | 5 | TRAMPOLINE | 60 |
| CLAW-FOOTED BATH TUB | 100 | GORILLA MASK | 15 |
| CLOCK HANDS | 25 | 1938 MODEL 'Q' CAR | 250 |
| ROWBOAT | 75 | WEATHER VANE | 50 |
| GRANDFATHER CLOCK | 235 | BOWLING BALL | 25 |
| 5 SPEED YO-YO | 5 | SUN DIAL | 10 |
| BIRCHBARK CANOE | 210 | RACING TROPHY | 500 |
| NEEDLE-NOSE PLIERS | 1 | CHRISTMAS CAKE | 50 |
| PHONE BOOTH | 100 | FIREMAN'S HAT | 5 |
| PURPLE COW | 150 | ALL-DAY SUCKER | 10 |
| FULL-LENGTH MIRROR | 20 | LACERTILIA SQUAMATA | 2000 |

Bingo was about to leave when he noticed the two reptiles standing nearby.

"Hey, Catchum!" said Bingo. "Who do you think is going to win? Dotty? Montgomery? Zipper?"

"Me," said Catchum, coolly polishing the buttons on his jacket.

"You can't be serious!" exclaimed Bingo. He could not believe that anyone but a member of the Get Along Gang could win the Scavenger Hunt.

"If you are serious," said Bingo suddenly, "let's make a bet. If one of the Get Along Gang wins, then you have to clean our clubhouse for a whole year."

"Agreed," said Catchum. "But if *I* win, you have to give me the clubhouse!"

"You're on," said Bingo. "The Get Along Gang just can't be beat."

When Bingo was gone, Leland looked at Catchum grumpily. "Why did you say we'd clean the clubhouse, Boss?" he asked. "I don't want to clean anything."

"Don't worry," said Catchum. "You won't have to. We're going to win the Scavenger Hunt. You see, I added a difficult item to the list—a lacertilia squamata. It's worth two thousand points, and I'm the only contestant who will find one."

"Well, come on!" cried Leland. "Let's go get the lacerelli spaghetti." Leland rushed forward, but a large reptilian arm reached out and drew him back.

"Slow down, Leland," said Catchum. "You're overworking your legs. We don't have to find anything. Lacertilia squamata is just a fancy scientific name for lizard."

"Ohhhh," said Leland, nodding slowly. "I get it." The fact was, however, that Leland didn't understand Catchum at all.

"At last," said Catchum, stretching out in the sun. "Now let me take my morning nap."

While Catchum caught a little shut-eye, Leland came up with an idea. For once, he would show Catchum how smart he really was. He would go find a lizard by himself.

There was other activity in Green Meadow that morning. Bleachers for the Grand Prix Race had been set up near the Sweets Factory, and spectators were busy buying tickets and finding their seats. Drivers were busy shining up their cars and checking the engines. The Green Meadow Marching Band did its part by performing some fancy maneuvers before the big race.

Elsewhere in Green Meadow, the Get Along Gang was involved in fancy maneuvers of its own. Montgomery had located a claw-footed bathtub, worth one hundred points, at the dump. He was trying to maneuver it onto his small red wagon.

In another part of the dump, Dotty had found an air compressor pump. She was trying to pull it free so she could hoist it into her wheelbarrow.

Rudyard was at the edge of the pond trying to paddle the rowboat he had found, plus Woolma and her full-length mirror. Woolma was simply trying to see herself in the mirror.

Alongside the boat was a sundial carried by Rocco Rabbit. The sundial was worth ten points, and Rocco was skating hard to rush it back to Hoofnagel's.

Zipper, absorbed in thoughts of winning, sailed along happily on his motorized scooter, balancing a canoe on the handlebars. Suddenly it dawned on him that he could not see where he was going.

At that moment Zipper was headed for a narrow gap between two trees. Amazingly, his scooter zipped right through. Not surprisingly, Zipper and the canoe did not.

Zipper's scooter banged into Dotty's wheelbarrow.

Dotty's pump was carried away by the passing scooter.

The wheelbarrow rolled in a circle and scooped Dotty up. It hit a bump and threw Dotty into the air.

She landed in one end of Zipper's canoe, sending Zipper flying.

The canoe slid down the hill like a toboggan, sideswiped Dotty's wheelbarrow, and crashed into Montgomery's bathtub.

Dottie and Zipper had just found their own vehicles when suddenly Montgomery's red wagon began to roll downhill again. The runaway race continued.

Meanwhile, back at the Ice Cream Emporium, Catchum was waking up. "Well, Leland," he said with a yawn, glancing up at the town clock, "there's no need to hurry yet. I'm sure the Get Along Gang is still racing around Green Meadow, while we rest our bones. Right, Leland? Leland? LE-LAND??"

Not long after Catchum discovered that Leland was missing, Catchum too was racing around Green Meadow, searching frantically for the lacertilia squamata.

Where *was* Leland? He was standing by a stone wall, looking for lizards. He was also standing in the way of a number of strange vehicles that were coming straight at him: an out-of-control bathtub, a speeding rowboat, a high-powered wheelbarrow, and a scooter driven by a canoe. The traffic was racing for the small opening in the wall. Leland barely had time to duck out of the way before everyone reached the opening at the same moment.

After the crash, there was silence. Zipper was holding Woolma's mirror. Woolma was sitting on Zipper's canoe. Rocco had Rudyard's rowboat. Rudyard was staring blankly at Rocco's sundial.

Just then, Braker Turtle bounced past on an electric pogo stick. He was wearing a gorilla mask. "Forty-five points!" shouted the gang, and everyone began scrambling for their things.

"Hey, give me back my sundial!" cried Rocco.
"Well, you've got my rowboat," replied Rudyard.
Montgomery and Dotty shook their heads sadly.

Montgomery shouted above the others. "Wait a minute!" he said. "Let's take it easy and try to help each other. After all, we are the Get Along Gang."

The group turned and stared at Montgomery as if he had just arrived from Mars.

"That's right," said Dotty. "We can sort this stuff out calmly and be on our way in no time."

The gang stared at Dotty as if she lived on Jupiter.

Suddenly Catchum ran by, calling, "Lee-land, where are you? Time is running out."

At the mention of time, the contestants started shouting and grabbing things again. Montgomery and Dotty heaved a sigh. At last everyone was back on the road to Hoofnagel's.

Leland crawled out from behind the stone wall. "Nope," he said. "No lizards back there." Leland was still blissfully unaware that Catchum was searching for him.

At the ice-cream store, the bins were filling up. There was only one hour left. After Zipper brought in his canoe, he managed to find a grandfather clock. The clock was worth two hundred and thirty-five points. Zipper was winning.

Flora Fox brought in a lampshade and a ball of tin foil.

Woolma and Rudyard brought in a purple cow. Montgomery found a weather vane.

Portia drove up on her tricycle, proud of the tambourine she had found. "I'm sorry, Portia," said Officer Growler. "The list doesn't say tambourine. It says trampoline."

"Oh, no," said Portia. "*I'll* never win."

By this time, Dotty had made an extraordinary discovery. Someone in Green Meadow owned an old 1938 Model Q, the very automobile named on the Scavenger Hunt list.

"If you can get it to run," said the owner, "you can have it for the day. Nobody has bothered to fix the car since it broke down in 1939."

"Fixing things is my specialty," said Dotty. She took some tools out of her toolbox and started to work.

The entire Get Along Gang happened to be standing in front of Hoofnagel's when Dotty approached in the Model Q. *Pa-chug. Pa-chug. Pong.* The car was making queer noises.

"It's barely holding together," Dotty said to herself, "but it has to make it to Hoofnagel's."

"Two hundred and fifty points for Dotty Dog!" said Officer Growler as the Model Q chugged up to the Emporium. Then it sputtered, coughed once, and stopped dead.

Catchum was staring gloomily into his empty bin when he heard a voice behind him. "I'm sorry I couldn't find a liz—"

At the sound of Leland's voice, Catchum whirled around. "Oh, Leland, my long lost lizard!" he cried. He threw his arms around Leland and gave him an enormous hug. Then he grabbed him by the tail and plopped him into the bin.

"This little lacertilia squamata here gives me two thousand points!" said Catchum gleefully. "I win."

The Get Along Gang turned and stared at Catchum. Then they stared at Leland Lizard. Dotty Dog broke the silence.

"Lacertilia squamata means lizard?" she said. Catchum nodded happily.

"You must have cheated," said Zipper. "Catchum, I think you put that last item on the list yourself. Well, I can cheat too."

"Wait a minute, Zipper," said Montgomery. "The Get Along Gang doesn't cheat to win contests."

"We'll have another chance at the Scavenger Hunt next year," added Dotty.

Bingo gulped. "We'll have another clubhouse by then too," he said, his voice heavy with gloom.

It was Bingo's turn to be stared at by the gang. "I bet Catchum that he wouldn't win," Bingo explained apologetically. "I was so sure he wouldn't win that I bet him the…clubhouse."

"You did what?" cried Zipper.

"We're doomed," said Bingo sadly, "unless one of us has more than two thousand points."

"I have an idea," said Montgomery. "If we add all our points together, we might have enough to beat Catchum. Let's put everything we've collected into…Zipper's bin. He was winning anyway." Zipper smiled an embarrassed but happy smile.

The gang went to work. Rudyard helped Montgomery carry the bathtub. Montgomery helped Rudyard carry the rowboat. Everyone worked together.

"Hmmm," said Catchum nervously, watching from a distance. "There's a slight chance that the Get Along Gang will win after all. I always knew there was something about cooperation I didn't like."

Braker Turtle tallied up the points carefully. "We need about five hundred more to beat Catchum," he said.

"The Grand Prix silver cup is worth five hundred points," said Woolma. "And it's very pretty too."

Catchum began to chortle. "The Grand Prix race hasn't started yet, hee, hee," he said, giggling. "Why don't you go over to the, ho, ho, racetrack and win it? Ha, ha."

"We would, if we had a car," said Bingo defiantly.

"We do have a car," declared Dotty. "We have the Model Q. Of course, it's not running at the moment, but..."

"You can get it going again, Dotty," said Bingo. "But we have to hurry. The race is about to start."

"Well, if Montgomery steered," said Dotty, "and everyone else pushed, I could go to work on the engine."

Montgomery jumped into the driver's seat. Dotty disappeared under the hood, and the gang slowly pushed the old car down the street in the direction of the bleachers. Catchum watched them go, laughing hysterically.

When the Get Along Gang reached the Grand Prix starting line, the other cars were already in position. The gang quickly parked the Model Q behind them. Dotty still hadn't been able to get the motor going.

The announcer's voice came over the loudspeaker. "The cars are warming up, and in just a minute...whoa! What's this coming onto the track? It looks as if we have a last-minute entry in today's big race."

Dotty was still under the hood, tightening, loosening, listening for some sign of life.

"The flag is down!" said the announcer. "The race is on."

All the cars sped off except the Model Q.

"We have to help Dotty," said Montgomery.

Zipper put in high-octane gas. Bingo added oil. Portia cleaned the windshield. Finally there was nothing for the gang to do but sit in the car and wait for Dotty.

"What a car," Zipper said. "It went in for a pit stop before it began the race."

"They're passing the Sweets Factory," said the announcer. "It's Blue Lightning in the lead...followed by Four-wheel Beast and Red Rocket...."

Finally Dotty slid out from under the hood, gave Montgomery the thumbs-up signal, and hopped in the car. Montgomery turned on the ignition and stepped on the gas. VARRROOOM! The engine roared into action, and the car zoomed down the road.

Dotty fell over onto Bingo as they screeched around a curve. "Well, we may not win," said Dotty, "but we're having a good time."

The old Model Q had been saving up power for many years, and it was speedy that day. Soon it was whizzing by the Sweets Factory and on to the Old Haunted Badger Mansion.

As the car neared the covered bridge, the gang saw the other race cars ahead.

"It's the Four-wheel Beast, Blue Lightning, Red Rocket—and the Model Q!" said the astounded announcer.

The cars were coming around the last long stretch. "We're gaining on them, Montgomery," cried Dotty. "Floor it!"

"I am," said Montgomery. "I have been—the whole way!" The Model Q was still closing in on the leaders. The gang hung on for dear life. The old car roared up behind the pack. Montgomery tried to squeeze through to the front.

"It's the Rocket and Lightning," said the frantic announcer. "No. It's the Model Q and Lightning. Rocket. Model Q. Lightning…"

The race was wildly close. Just before the finish, the Model
Q hit a bump, and the gang flew into the air.

When they came down, Portia was driving. Montgomery was
sprawled on the hood of the car.

"Keep going, Portia!" cried Montgomery.

"I can't reach the pedal!" said Portia. Bingo moved over and
slapped his flat tail down on the gas pedal. The Model Q sped
to the finish line with Montgomery hanging onto the hood.

"...and it's the Model Q!" the announcer shouted. "By a moose's antler!"

The crowd in the bleachers cheered for the gang. Inside the car, Bingo was so excited, he forgot to take his tail off the pedal. The old car whizzed by the trophy table, and the Grand Prix cup caught on Montgomery's antler.

"I've got five hundred points on my antlers," said Montgomery with a grin. "Back to Hoofnagel's, Portia, like gangbusters!"

The gang survived the trip back to the Ice Cream Emporium. Officer Growler was waiting for the gang and quickly tallied up the final score. "Adding five hundred more points for the Grand Prix cup," he said at last, "the Get Along Gang wins with two thousand and one points!"

The town clock began to play its noon-hour chime. The Scavenger Hunt was over. All the members of the gang hugged each other and jumped up and down. Portia even hugged Mr. Hoofnagel.

That afternoon the Get Along Gang sat in Hoofnagel's, drinking all the milk shakes they could drink.

"Mr. Hoofnagel," said Woolma, batting her long eyelashes, "it is extremely generous of you to treat us *all* to free milk shakes."

"My mistake," said crochety old Mr. Hoofnagel. "And, by the way, the new name of my purple ice cream is Get Along Grape."

Catchum and Leland were not celebrating in Hoofnagel's. They were off on a new scavenger hunt—to find a mop and a broom.

"What a day this has been!" said Dotty. "Imagine, winning the Grand Prix, the Scavenger Hunt, a year's worth of clubhouse cleanings, and forty-five milk shakes—so far—all in one morning! How did we do it?"

"How did we do it?" said Montgomery cheerfully. "We did it together."

"Get Along Gang, what do you say?
Getting along is the only way.
Get Along Gang, let's hear the call.
All for one, and one for all!"